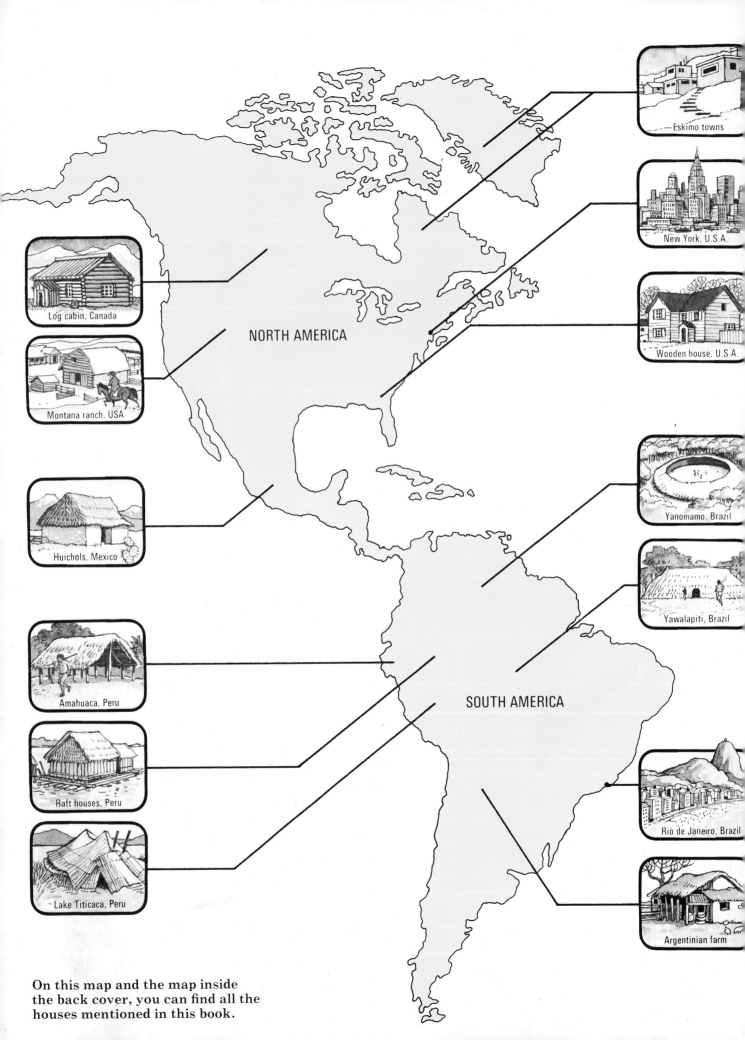

Eskimo towns

New York, U.S.A.

Wooden house, U.S.A.

Log cabin, Canada

Montana ranch, USA

NORTH AMERICA

Yanomamo, Brazil

Huichols, Mexico

Yawalapiti, Brazil

Amahuaca, Peru

SOUTH AMERICA

Raft houses, Peru

Rio de Janeiro, Brazil

Lake Titicaca, Peru

Argentinian farm

On this map and the map inside
the back cover, you can find all the
houses mentioned in this book.

Chalets

HOUSES AND HOMES

Round houses

Carol Bowyer

Illustrated by Bob Hersey, Rob McCaig and Joseph McEwan

Designed by Graham Round

Edited by Lisa Watts

Houseboats

Farmhouses

Mud huts

Contents

Amazon jungle houses

ats being built

Lapp tents

Consultant editor: Dr Peter Loizos, Lecturer in Social Anthropology at London School of Economics, University of London, England. Additional designs by Anna Barnard.

Yurts

Reed houses

City houses

Grass huts

Stilt houses

Caravans

Caves

Houses through the ages

1 About 350,000 years ago

In prehistoric times people hunted wild animals for food. They often followed the animals from place to place and camped a few days in huts built from branches and grass.

2 About 7,000 years ago

Later, when people learned how to plant crops and tame animals, they no longer needed to hunt. They settled down and built more solid houses. Some used mud baked hard by the sun.

3 About 3,500 years ago

Gradually the villages grew and became towns. In this crowded ci in ancient Egypt, people lived in houses four or five storeys tall, as they were short of building space. They paid specially trained

5 About 900 years ago

In the early Middle Ages, country people lived in cottages made of "wattle and daub". They made a wooden frame and then filled it in with woven sticks (the wattle) and mud paste (the daub).

6 About 900 years ago

The Normans, who came from France, used stone for building. Their houses had outside staircases. You can spot a Norman building by its rounded door and window arches.

7 About 600 years ago

Town houses in the Middle Ages were built very close together. The upstairs rooms overhung the street and almost touched. There were no drains and people threw their rubbish into the street.

An Egyptian room

Egyptian houses, especially wealthy people's, were large and spacious. Small, high windows let in light and cool breezes, but kept out the glare of the hot summer sun. Guests were entertained in this hall.

Inside a peasant's cottage

Forests covered much of Europe in the Middle Ages, so wood was used for houses, furniture and even plates and bowls.

Cottage floors were bare earth, trodden down hard and animals shared the living room. The fire mad the room smoky.

...uilders to construct their houses,
...sing sun-dried bricks made of
...ud and chopped straw. The
...ricks were smoothed over with
...thin mixture of mud and water
...nd sometimes painted.

3 About 150 years ago

...hen machines and factories were
...vented, thousands of workers
...oved to the cities. Rows of
...ick houses, with small back
...rds and outside toilets, were
...ilt for them to live in.

About 2,000 years ago

4

Walls cut away so you can see inside

Stairs to bedroom

Main living room

Bedroom

Kitchen

Dining room diners lay on couches

Fireplace for under-floor heating

Slaves gardening

Wealthy Romans lived in large
villas like this. Whole streets of
Roman houses have been found at
Pompeii in Italy. They were
preserved in ash from the volcano
Vesuvius. These houses show that
the Romans made bricks and roof
tiles from clay baked in a fire,
and that they had under-floor,
hot-air central heating, baths and
inside toilets.

A Norman hall

Wooden shutter

...orman houses were cold
...d draughty because
...ey had no glass in the
...ndows. The only heat
...me from a log fire in a
huge stone fireplace in
the wall. This is the hall
where everyone ate and
slept. The kitchen was in
a separate building.

An old kitchen

Factory workers' houses
a hundred years ago had
no bathrooms. People
washed in tin baths in the
kitchen. They heated
water on the cooking
stove, which had a wood
or coal fire burning inside
it. Oil or gas lamps lit
their rooms.

Mud huts and round houses

In hot, dry countries, mud is still used for building houses. It is mixed with straw to bind it together and either made into bricks or moulded into walls. The sun bakes the mud rock-hard. In many parts of the world it is a good, easy-to-find material for building with.

Many of the village houses in Africa are built of mud. They are cool inside because the thick mud walls keep out the sun. Mud houses are often round, because their walls are less likely to crack than if they had corners.

Plan of Nabdam house

Mud village

Mud huts in Botswana have wide thatched roofs to keep rain off the walls. Some people have built cement houses and bought modern furniture, such as beds, which do not fit in the round houses.

These round mud huts are the homes of a people called the Nabdam who live in northern Ghana. Each family owns a group of huts joined by walls, and when the sons marry, new rooms are added for their wives. The women usually decorate the houses, by making grooves in the mud and painting them with coloured vegetable juices.

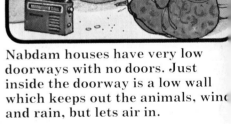

Nabdam houses have very low doorways with no doors. Just inside the doorway is a low wall which keeps out the animals, wind and rain, but lets air in.

Bushmen

In the Kalahari Desert in southern Africa, there are Bushmen who still live by hunting. They camp at night in small, round huts built of sticks and grass.

1 Moving to the city

Making an animal from a vegetable

Many Africans are now moving to the cities, where they hope to find jobs and earn more money. Houses are too expensive for them to buy when they first arrive. In some cities, they can buy a plot of land with piped water and a toilet and build a mud house. Later on, when they can afford it, they can have a modern cement house buil

asai houses

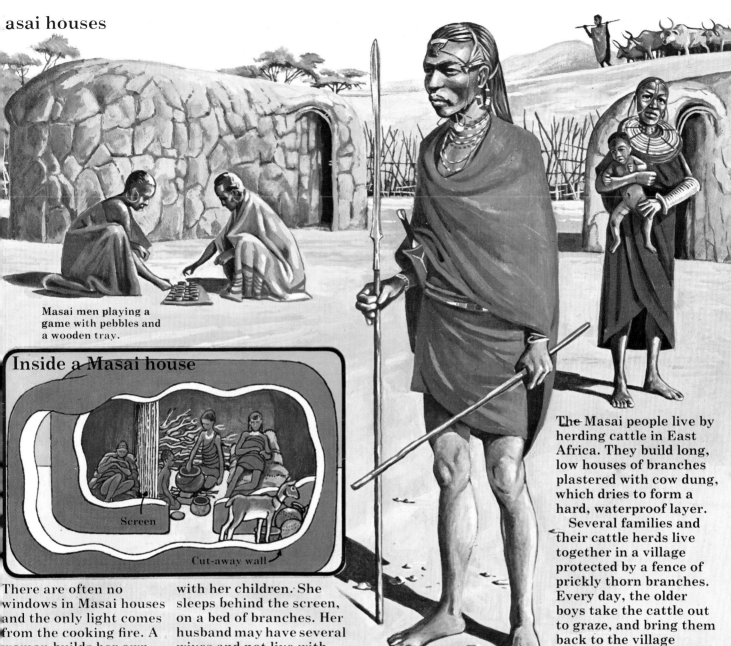

Masai men playing a game with pebbles and a wooden tray.

Inside a Masai house

Screen

Cut-away wall

There are often no windows in Masai houses and the only light comes from the cooking fire. A woman builds her own house and lives there with her children. She sleeps behind the screen, on a bed of branches. Her husband may have several wives and not live with her all the time.

The Masai people live by herding cattle in East Africa. They build long, low houses of branches plastered with cow dung, which dries to form a hard, waterproof layer.

Several families and their cattle herds live together in a village protected by a fence of prickly thorn branches. Every day, the older boys take the cattle out to graze, and bring them back to the village before nightfall.

In this busy street in an African town, here are mud houses with thatched roofs, side-by-side with modern blocks of flats. The mud houses are probably he homes of newcomers to the city.

Some of the houses now have iron roofs instead of thatch, because they do not need repairing so often. Iron-roofed houses are hot inside though, because the metal heats up in the sun.

Vegetable animals

Here are some ideas for making animals from vegetables, as the boy in picture 1 is doing.

WASP CARROT — PAINT STRIPES

HOOPS OF WIRE COVERED WITH SELLOTAPE

USED MATCHSTICKS

POTATO HEDGEHOG

STICK IN PINS OR MATCHES POINTING BACKWARDS

SCREWS OR NAILS FOR EYES

Living in the jungle

Jungle, or rainforest, is hot and steamy and thick with plants and trees which grow very large because it rains heavily nearly every day. People who live there have to clear away the jungle growth before they can build houses or plant crops.

Much of the world's jungle has been cut down to make space for cities and farms. The largest jungle is around the Amazon river, in South America, where most of the people shown here live.

Giant round house

Deep in the Amazon jungle in Brazil and Venezuela, the Yanomamo Indians live under great circular roofs, like this. As many as 125 people live under each roof.

Inside a Yanomamo house

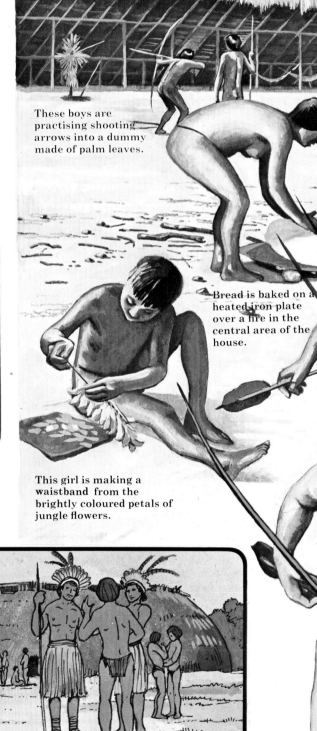

These boys are practising shooting arrows into a dummy made of palm leaves.

Bread is baked on a heated iron plate over a fire in the central area of the house.

This girl is making a waistband from the brightly coloured petals of jungle flowers.

With their faces smeared with war paint, these boys are pretending to raid an enemy camp as their fathers used to do.

Palm leaf houses

The Yawalapiti Indians of Brazil live in large palm-thatched houses in clearings in the jungle. About 30 people live together in one house and there are four or more houses in each village. The houses have no windows so they are dark and stuffy inside. The Yawalapiti live by hunting, fishing and growing a few crops.

Pygmy hunters' leaf huts

The Mbuti people live in the jungle in Zaire, Africa. They are Pygmies, a race of people who are only about 130cm tall. They live mainly by hunting and gathering.

At night they sleep in round huts made of branches and sticks covered with large jungle leaves. The leaves keep out the rain, but easily catch fire when dry, so the Mbuti light fires outside their houses. On cold nights they sleep outside beside the fire.

he Yanomamo people sleep in ammocks and store their few ossessions in the roof. Each anomamo family has its own ea under the roof. The roof is ade from the leaves of palm trees, id in layers over a framework of

poles. Cool breezes blow in through a narrow gap between the roof and the ground. About every two years, when the roof starts to leak or is full of insects, the Yanomamo burn it down and build a new one.

Jungle houses in Peru

hese Amahuaca people f Peru are cutting back e jungle to make a earing where they will it up a new house.

They lash sticks together to build a wooden frame which they thatch with palm leaves.

This Amahuaca woman is making a pot from coils of clay. Women plant and harvest the crops and also prepare the food.

This is a small jungle town on the Amazon river. The houses are built on stilts or rafts to protect them from floods.

7

Tents and caravans

Wooden pins

Cheese made from goats' milk drying in the sun.

Bedding

Churning milk in a goatskin to turn it to butter.

Pounding coffee beans to fine grains for making small cups of bitter black coffee.

Flour and water dough being made into flat loaves of bread.

Grinding wheat to make flour.

Some Bedouin keep a few hens for their eggs.

The Bedouin are Arabs who wander across the Arabian desert, herding camels, goats and sheep. They live in tents made of cloth woven from goat hair. Each tent has a dividing curtain.

On one side is the women's area where the family sleeps and the women cook. On the other side, the men receive their guests and hold meetings. When men from outside the family visit the tent, all the women hide. They hang another curtain from the tent rope so the men cannot see into their part of the tent.

Gypsy caravans

This gypsy family are camping beside the road in their horse-drawn caravan. Gypsies are descended from travelling people who came from India. Now they live all over Europe and the Middle East.

In this caravan there is an old-fashioned wood-burning stove for cooking. Cupboards and walls have traditional decorations.

Most gypsies now live in modern caravans. They camp by the roads or on special gypsy campsites.

The side cloths are pinned to the roof and can be lifted to let in the breeze.

Coffee pot

Coffee cups

Inside the tent, the Bedouin sit on carpets. They have no furniture. When the guests arrive they bring out cushions for them to sit on.

How to make a tent

Here are some ideas for making tents indoors and outside.

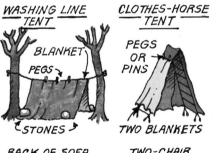

WASHING LINE TENT

CLOTHES-HORSE TENT

BLANKET

PEGS

PEGS OR PINS

STONES

TWO BLANKETS

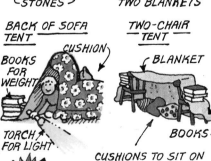

BACK OF SOFA TENT

TWO-CHAIR TENT

CUSHION

BOOKS FOR WEIGHT

BLANKET

TORCH FOR LIGHT

BOOKS

CUSHIONS TO SIT ON

NEVER light a fire inside your tent.

These are some useful things for making tents: broomsticks, blankets, safety pins, books, cushions, stones.

1 Living in yurts

The Turcoman live in the desert in Iran, travelling from place to place in search of water and pastures. They live in tents called yurts, which they carry with them on their camels.

The Turcoman women pitch the yurts. They put up a wooden frame first, then cover it with pieces of felt. In winter they use several layers of felt to keep out the cold.

There are three areas inside the yurt: one for sleeping, one for the women and one for the men. The bedding is stored in the sleeping area at the back of the tent.

Clothes and cooking pots are hung on the women's side. Weaving equipment, bags of wheat and flour, saddles and guns are kept on the men's side.

Turcoman women make the felt for covering the yurts, and for carpets and saddle bags too. The felt is made from sheep's wool. The young girls comb out the wool. Then the women wet it and roll

and press it between reed mats until the wool becomes tangled and matted to form felt. They make carpets and bags with coloured patterns, but wall felts are white until fire smoke blackens them.

Ranches and farmhouses

Thatched farmhouse

This painted English farmhouse has changed very little since it was built about 300 years ago. It was made of local stone and thatched with straw. The farmer and his family still live in it. The cowsheds, barns for hay, animal feed and farm machinery surround the yard. Many farms are in the middle of their fields, away from other houses.

A Danish farmhouse

Old farmhouses in Denmark, like this one, were once the home of the farmer, his family and his animals. Now sheds and stables have been built for pigs, cattle, hay and machinery, round a yard at the back of the house. The animals are kept indoors from October to May when it is too cold for grazing. This farmhouse also has rooms for farm workers and summer guests.

Spanish farming village

Farmhouses in Spain are often built close together on the steep hillsides. This leaves the flat land in the valley clear for farming. On the ground floor are stables and a grape press for making wine. The farmer and his family live on the next floor. The top floor is used for store rooms.

A farm in Argentina

In the countryside round the city of Cordoba, in Argentina, farmers have small houses built of mud bricks (sometimes called "adobe"). This farmhouse is surrounded by a fence to form a yard called a corral, where cattle, pigs and hens are kept at night. In the corral there is an oven, where the farmer's wife bakes her bread, and a well which provides drinking water. The farmer owns a small plot of land nearby where he grows vegetables and a few orange trees.

Farmers coming home from fields.

Grapevines

Drying sheep's wool

Drying vegetables

1 Life on a sheep station

Windmill

Sheep farms on the dry grasslands of Australia cover thousands of square kilometres. Farming families are often more than a day's drive from their nearest neighbours. Water has to be pumped up from underground streams by windmills. Supplies and letters come by plane.

Ranch-hands often ride motorbikes now, instead of horses, when they round up the sheep. They are helped by sheepdogs.

Children living on remote stations have lessons by two-way radio. They write their homework and post it to their teachers.

1 On a cattle ranch

n the Rocky Mountains, in Montana, U.S.A., cattle ranches re huge. In winter, hay is taken y horse-drawn sledges to feed the attle. The cowboys live in wooden bunk houses near the ranch house. They now drive the cattle to market in large trucks, rather than herding them along the old cattle trails.

In spring the cowboys take the cattle up to the mountains looking for grass for grazing. They live in wooden cabins and cook over campfires.

Living on water

The Bajau people live on boats which they sail round the islands of South-East Asia. They are sometimes called sea gypsies.

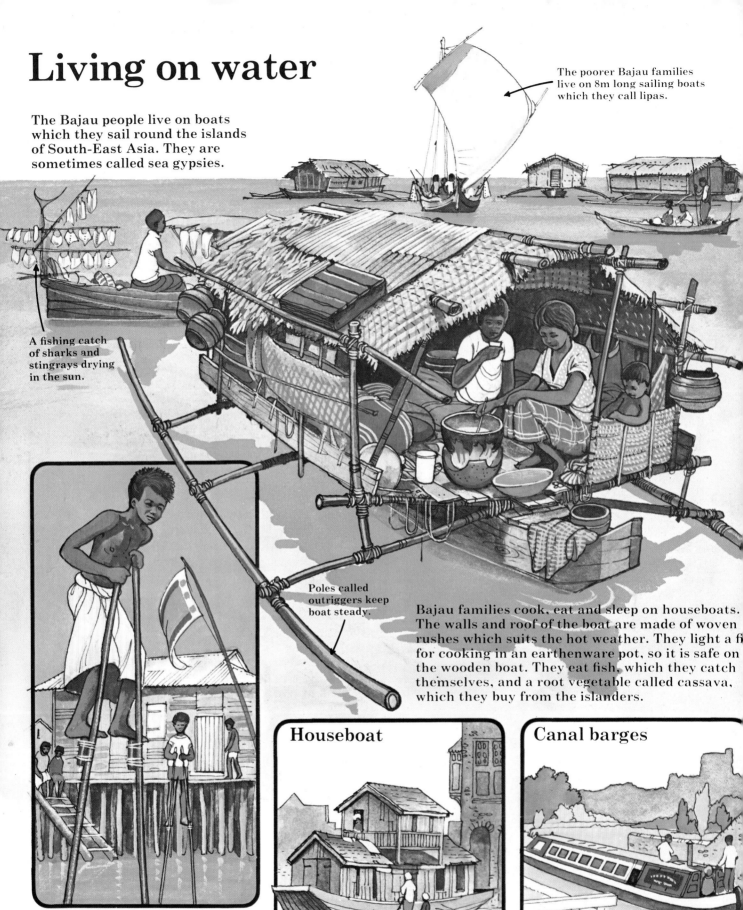

The poorer Bajau families live on 8m long sailing boats which they call lipas.

A fishing catch of sharks and stingrays drying in the sun.

Poles called outriggers keep boat steady.

Bajau families cook, eat and sleep on houseboats. The walls and roof of the boat are made of woven rushes which suits the hot weather. They light a fi for cooking in an earthenware pot, so it is safe on the wooden boat. They eat fish, which they catch themselves, and a root vegetable called cassava, which they buy from the islanders.

Some Bajaus now live in houses built on stilts along the coast. They still go out fishing though some also earn a living by farming. These children are using stilts to walk between the houses.

Houseboat

Some people in Kashmir in north India live on houseboats moored on the lakes. They row to land in small boats and do their shopping from shopboats.

Canal barges

In Europe, whole families used to live on the barges that transported goods along the canals. Today they are used mainly as holiday homes.

Houses in the marshes

On the vast marshlands between the Tigris and Euphrates rivers in southern Iraq, live people known as Marsh Arabs. They keep buffaloes, grow rice and catch fish in the lagoons.

Reed fence

Island of reeds and mud

Building a new house

Building a boat

Children playing with water buffaloes.

Drying buffalo dung which will be used for fuel.

Women cooking

The Marsh Arabs build their houses with reeds. There is little firm land in the marshes, so first they have to make an island, by fencing off part of the swamp and filling it in with rushes and mud.

Building a reed house

1

Bundles of giant reeds, cut from the marshes, are tied together and bent into a framework for the house. Ancient carvings show that this method of building was used here over 5,000 years ago.

2

Weaving wall mats

The walls and roofs of the Marsh Arabs' houses are made of mats woven from reeds. They sell spare mats in the local village markets. New wall mats have to be woven every few years as the reeds rot.

3

The houses are quite warm in winter as the matting keeps out the wind. Warmth from the fire dries out the reeds. In summer the walls are rolled up to let in the breeze.

13

Tree houses

In this look out, 12m up in the trees, men in India watched for enemies. Tree houses are not used as permanent homes, because it is very difficult to get water, food and firewood from the ground to the house. They are also easy for enemies to beseige or burn down.

Among some tribal peoples in New Guinea, young unmarried girls sometimes had to live in tree houses, and special ceremonies were held in them. Some even had fireplaces inside, made of clay or stone so they did not burn the house down.

Tree-stump house

The stump of this giant redwood tree has made a good solid platform for a house. It is used as a holiday house by its American owners.

Tree hide-out

This tree is big enough for four people to sit inside comfortably.

Baobab trees have extremely thick trunks. This one, which is in Africa, was hollowed out a long time ago as a hiding place during a war between two tribes. Since then, hunters have often sheltered in it and now it is a local landmark.

Building a tree house

If you want to build a treehouse, remember, it could damage the tree, so you should ask permission of the tree's owner first. If you live near an adventure playground, you could ask the playground leader if you could build a treehouse there. Never take candles or light a fire in a treehouse.

Living in caves

In 1971 a forest hunter called Dafal discovered some people called the Tasaday, living in caves in a remote valley in the Philippines. The entrances to their caves were high up in the rocks. To reach them they climbed trees or swung across on the long, rope-like stems of jungle plants.

Bamboo tube full of water

When Dafal found them, the Tasaday were wearing clothes made from leaves, and using stone tools. They lived on wild plants and flowers, grubs, lizards, crabs and snakes.

1 Cave houses in Turkey

Pigeon houses

This strange landscape of cone-shaped rocks is in Turkey. The rock is soft and easy to carve, and for over 2,000 years local people have built their houses, churches and monasteries in the rocks. They hollowed out the cones and put in wooden windows and doors. When the rock is exposed to the air, it hardens.

2

Inside their cave homes, the people cover the earth floors with carpets and paint the rocky walls. They have carved rock staircases which lead to more rooms upstairs.

French caves

These old caves in France have been made into modern homes by building on new fronts with windows and doors and adding chimneys.

High in the mountains

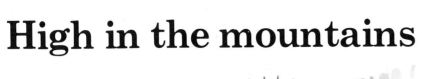

There are people living in even the highest mountain ranges of the world. It is cold and desolate there and they need sturdy, thick-walled houses to protect them.

These are prayer flags, h[...]
on the roof to bring good luck.

Firewood is stored here on the roof.

Poorer families use oiled paper instead of glass in the windows.

This girl is spinning a prayer wheel as she recites prayers of the Buddhist religion.

This is the only doorway everyone has to go through the yak stable to get into the house.

These are the Lobas people, who live among the snow-capped peaks of the Himalayas in Nepal. The highest mountain in the world, Mount Everest, is not far away. There are no trees to shelter them from the wind, because it is too cold for them to grow.

This family's house is built of stone and mud-brick. The ground floor is used as a stable and heat from the animals' bodies helps keep the house warm. The people live upstairs. They farm a few crops and keep sheep, goats, and mountain animals called yaks.

Yaks carry heavy loads an[...] pull ploughs. Their hair is used for clothing and their dung for fuel. The females called dris, supply milk, butter and cheese.

1 Mexican mountain farm

The Huichols are American Indians who live in the mountains of western Mexico. It gets bitterly cold in winter, though trees and cacti still grow there. They live in isolated family groups on farms called "ranchos", several hours' walk from each other. Here, the Huichols are holding a ceremony to wish the men good luck when they travel into the mountains.

Good luck crosses

Inside the house, the family has a wood-burning stove for cooking food. There is also a bamboo churn for brewing tea, which they drink with butter and salt.

Some families now have more modern equipment, such as thermos flasks and pressure cookers. They buy these on rare trading expeditions to the towns.

This is a demon trap. The Lobas hang these over their doorways to keep away evil spirits. Round the ram's skull is a picture of each person living in the house.

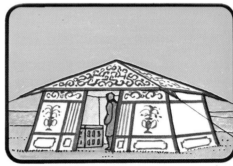

In summer, the Lobas leave their isolated houses and meet other families for parties and picnics. They camp in tents like this one.

The ranchos are groups of huts made from stone and adobe (mud bricks). The thatched roofs overhang the walls to protect them from heavy rain.

This hut is used for cooking. These Huichol are making "tortillas", thin flat pancakes made with maize, which they eat instead of bread or rice.

Good luck crosses

To make good luck crosses like the Huichols, you will need some straws and wool.

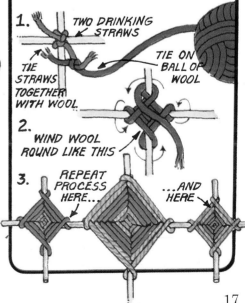

1. TWO DRINKING STRAWS
TIE STRAWS TOGETHER WITH WOOL
TIE ON BALL OF WOOL

2. WIND WOOL ROUND LIKE THIS

3. REPEAT PROCESS HERE... ...AND HERE

Wooden houses and log cabins

1 Swiss chalets

In Switzerland, houses built of wood, like the farmhouse shown above, are called chalets. In the mountains and forested valleys, most of the houses are wooden.

In winter, the ground floor is used as a stable. This part of the house is built of stone so the damp does not rot it. The snow on the gently sloping roof helps to keep heat in.

Almost everything inside the chalet is made of wood, so there are strict laws about fire safety. The windows have double layers of glass to keep the house warm.

Old Japanese farmhouse

Inside the Japanese farmhouse, the family sleeps on a wooden platform covered with straw mat. In the past, there were no stables and the animals slept in here too.

Trays of silkworms

This is an old-fashioned farmhouse in Japan. It is built of wood and thatched with reeds. There is no glass in the windows. Instead they are covered with screens made of straw and sliding wooden shutters which keep out the snow. The two small buildings in front of the house are where animals are kept. This is called a Minka farmhouse.

The attics are mainly used for growing silkworms. At both ends there are windows to let in the sunlight.

18

Haystacks

Winter houses
in valley

Firewood

Cows wear
bells so their
owners can
find them.

In summer, when the snow melts,
the villagers move higher up the
mountains to find good grass for
their cows and to harvest hay
ready for the winter.

While they are there they live in
log cabins roofed with stones from
the mountain quarries. These are
much smaller and simpler than
their winter homes in the valleys.

They cut the long grass, stack it
and leave it to dry into hay. Before
the winter snows come they take
the hay and the animals back
down the mountain.

Building wooden houses

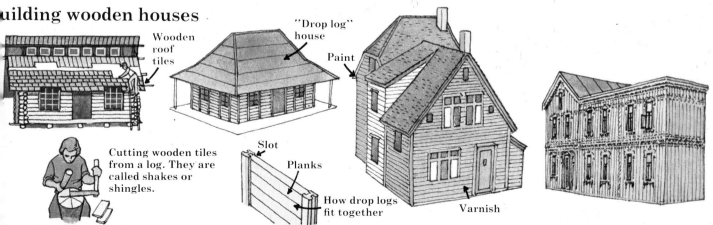

Wooden
roof
tiles

"Drop log"
house

Paint

Cutting wooden tiles
from a log. They are
called shakes or
shingles.

Slot

Planks

How drop logs
fit together

Varnish

This cabin is made of
logs which are fitted
together at the corners
in a criss-cross pattern.
It is being roofed with
wooden tiles.

In this house the planks
of wood are fitted into
slots in the upright
posts. These are called
"drop log" houses.

Wooden houses have to be
treated against insects
and painted or varnished
regularly, to prevent the
wood from rotting.

Some older wooden
houses are decorated
with carvings like this
one in eastern USSR.

Living in icy places

The coldest places on Earth are the arctic lands near the North Pole, and Antarctica, the land at the South Pole. The winters are very long and the summers are warm, but short. For most of the year the land and sea are covered with thick snow and ice. In winter, it is daylight for only a few hours each day, but in summer the days are very long.

The Lapps

The Lapps live in the arctic lands of Norway, Finland, Sweden and Russia. Their clothes are embroidered with different patterns depending on the area they come from.

In the past they lived by hunting and herding reindeer. Nowadays most Lapps live and work in small towns.

A few Lapp families still keep herds of reindeer. In spring, they leave their homes and travel with the animals to the coast to escape the heat and insects of summer. On the way, they live in tents which they carry with them on their sledges. Some Lapp herders now use snow-mobiles instead of sledges.

Inside a Lapp tent

Lapp herdsman lining his fur boots with dried grass to keep his feet warm.

Lapp tents are made from sticks covered with reindeer skins. The lay branches on the frozen grou inside the tent and cover them with fur rugs to keep out the col

1 Living in frozen Antarctica

Ice breaker supply ship

The only people who live in Antarctica are scientists and explorers. All their food and supplies have to be taken to them by ship or plane.

During the long winter no ships or planes can reach Antarctica. It is so cold and windy that the scientists cannot go outside.

2

This "Sno-cat" is going to a research station which is in a tunnel 10m down in the ice.

3

In spring, when th first ship breaks through the ice, it brings letters and parcels from hom

They carry supplies of dried food which they cook over the fire in the tent. At night they wrap themselves in reindeer skins and lie down near the fire. Some Lapps now have modern canvas tents.

1 Eskimo houses

Teams of husky dogs pull sledges

Seal skin being cleaned

Eskimos used to live by hunting seals and whales. Now most of them work in towns and go hunting in their spare time for seal skins to sell. They live in Greenland, and in northern Canada, Alaska and Russia.

In these freezing lands, the Eskimos build their houses of wood and line them with fibreglass so that they stay warm inside. They build on rocks or oil drums sunk in the ice so the houses stay firm if the surface ice melts.

2

In the past, when Eskimos went hunting, they lived in igloos which they built with blocks of snow. Nowadays the hunters take tents with them or stay in huts.

3

It was quite warm inside the igloos. The icy walls were covered with fur rugs. Lamps burning whale oil gave off heat and light.

Eskimo hunter

This Eskimo hunter is hiding behind a white screen so the animals cannot see him against the snow. The hunters use rifles now instead of spears.

An Eskimo game

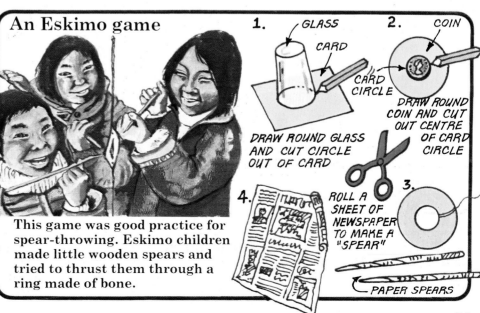

1. GLASS CARD
DRAW ROUND GLASS AND CUT CIRCLE OUT OF CARD

2. COIN CARD CIRCLE
DRAW ROUND COIN AND CUT OUT CENTRE OF CARD CIRCLE

3.

4. ROLL A SHEET OF NEWSPAPER TO MAKE A "SPEAR"

PAPER SPEARS

This game was good practice for spear-throwing. Eskimo children made little wooden spears and tried to thrust them through a ring made of bone.

Living together

Palm thatch roof

Bedding mats

Ladder carved from a log

A kibbutz

Children's house

Lessons outdoors

1 Chinese commune

These caves used to be houses, but are now pigsties.

A kibbutz is a village in Israel where everyone has a share in the land and property of the village. They work and eat together and meet to discuss kibbutz affairs. Sometimes children live in special houses, away from their parents.

Taichai village is part of a Chinese commune, where everyone works together on the land. They share the produce among themselves and with the other villages in the commune. Flat "terrace" have been cut into the hillsides to make farmla...

Washing clothes

Devil scares

Pounding rice

In the dense jungle on the island of Borneo, people called the Dayaks live in longhouses like this one. Between 20 and 50 families live in one house, which they all help to build. There are separate rooms for each family along the outside and an open space, like a street, down the centre. The Dayaks live near rivers and they build their longhouses on stilts.

Underground houses

Mosque where people go to pray

Air vent

At Matmata, on the edge of the Sahara Desert, people build their houses below the ground. They dig about 9m down into the soft rock. Several other desert peoples also do this because there are not enough stones or trees with which to build houses. Under the ground they can find water and shelter from sandstorms. It is cooler there too during the hot days.

Tunnel entrance

Store room

Tunnel leading to surface

Well

Oven

There is a central courtyard, open to the sky, which has doorways leading off into the underground rooms. Some of the rooms are for families to live in. Others are stables for their animals and storerooms where they keep grain to last them until the next harvest.

2

Fireplace

his is a store room, living room nd bedroom. The stone platform the family bed, which has a replace underneath to heat it in ld weather.

1 Tunnel homes

This is Coober Pedy, a small, hot, dusty town in southern Australia, where the average temperature in summer is 38°C. Most of the people are opal miners.

2

Some miners have made their homes in old mine tunnels. It is so much cooler there that tunnels are now being dug specially for living in.

Villages

A village on stilts

School house

Well

splitting a coconut

This isolated village in Malaysia is called a kampong. It is built in a jungle clearing, where it is often very hot and wet. The houses are built on stilts to let the air blow round them and keep them cool and dry. There are no roads or shops and there is no electricity. All the water comes from a well in the middle of the village. There is a village school and also a shelter where the women gather to make baskets.

Village in West Africa

Every day of the week there is a market in one of the villages in the dry lands of West Africa, on the edge of the Sahara Desert.

Vegetable garden

Basket of millet

Mud-brick house

Towers for storing millet

The land is so dry in this part of Africa that the people find it difficult to grow enough to eat. Every few years they move to find more fertile land, and their old mud houses crumble and disappear from sight.

Beer made from millet

Chillis

Millet

Families live in groups of huts, built round yards and surrounded by walls. A village is made up of lots of scattered family groups, each with its farming land round it.

In the rainy season, the women grow ground nuts, chillies and vegetables in gardens near their houses. If they grow more than their families can eat, they sell it at one of the markets.

1 Island village

2

In the Greek island of Santorini the houses are built close together on the hillside above the harbour. The flat land on the island is kept for farming.

In summer it gets very hot and the houses are painted white to reflect the sunlight. Most houses have two storeys and an outside staircase.

After the baker has baked the bread in the morning, villagers who do not have ovens bring their midday meals to be cooked while his oven is still hot.

Nuts

1 An Indian village

When the women go to fetch water from the well, they also do their washing. Then they do not have to carry so much water home and can talk while they work.

England

In this Indian village the houses are made of stone and mud and are built around courtyards, where the women spend most of their time. The people here are Hindus. In the Hindu religion every family belongs to a special group called a "caste" which lives in a different section of the village.

In many English villages the houses face on to a green. There is usually a public house where people can meet, and a village church. People used to live and work in villages but now most of them travel to towns to work.

Cities

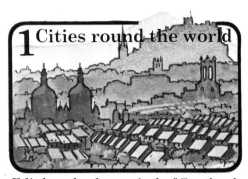

1 Cities round the world

Edinburgh, the capital of Scotland, grew up round a huge rock and castle where the people thought they would be safe from attack.

2

Eighty years ago Nairobi, in Kenya, was a village. When the railway was built, the city grew round it. Now giraffes in the Game Park can see modern blocks.

3

In the centre of New York are some of the highest skyscrapers in the world. The city began as a landing place for the first European settlers of America.

Living in cities

Some cities have grown over many centuries from villages or small towns. Others have grown up in just a few years. There is always a reason for a city to be where it is. People may have settled there because it was an easy place to defend from enemies, because it was a good centre for trade, or because it had the things needed for an industry.

1

In many cities, people live close together in old houses and flats. There are no gardens for children to play in.

2

On the edge of cities, richer people live in houses with gardens. They have to travel into the city centres to work.

3

There are not enough cheap houses in many cities. Poor people build shanty towns round them using wood, tin or mud.

4

So many people have moved into some cities, such as Calcutta in India, that there are no houses for them. They sleep in the streets.

5

Factories provide jobs for people but they may put smoke and dirt into the air. Travelling to them can be crowded and unpleasant.

6

Shop windows filled with radios, televisions and furniture bring visitors to cities. Some may stay, hoping to find work.

7

In cities there are hospitals and doctors. People come in from the countryside where there may be no doctors to care for them.

4 ...dney, on the coast of Australia, ...as founded where inlets made a ...atural, safe harbour. This is now ...ossed by ferries and a huge ...idge.

5 Cairo stands on the River Nile in Egypt, near the ancient pyramids of Giza. It is Africa's most crowded city. Every day more people come, looking for jobs.

6 Rio de Janeiro lies beneath Sugar Loaf Mountain on the coast of Brazil. It has fine houses on the beaches but shanty towns have been put up on the hillsides nearby.

New York street

During the hot summers in New York and other cities, many people sit, talk and play in the streets. It is cooler there than in their small flats and houses. The streets are closed to traffic on some special holidays and parties are held on the pavements and in the roads.

Parks in cities are pleasant places for people to walk and for children to play. The trees give shade for people to sit in and help to improve the air in smoky cities.

Adventure playgrounds have been built in some city centres, often on unused land. Here children can play and have fun, safe from the traffic on the roads.

Sports centres, stadiums and swimming pools are built in cities. Here, large numbers of people can watch and learn many sports.

Special places to live

Living on an oil rig

1 Fresh water and food have to be taken to the rig by boat. In rough seas, only helicopters can reach the rig.

2 Even in their cabins, the men can hear the constant noise of the drill. Every room has an alarm bell, in case of fire.

3 Workers on the drilling platform are called roughnecks. There is always someone working as the drill never stops.

Oil rigs are built on shore and towed out to sea. The legs are filled with water to make them sink.

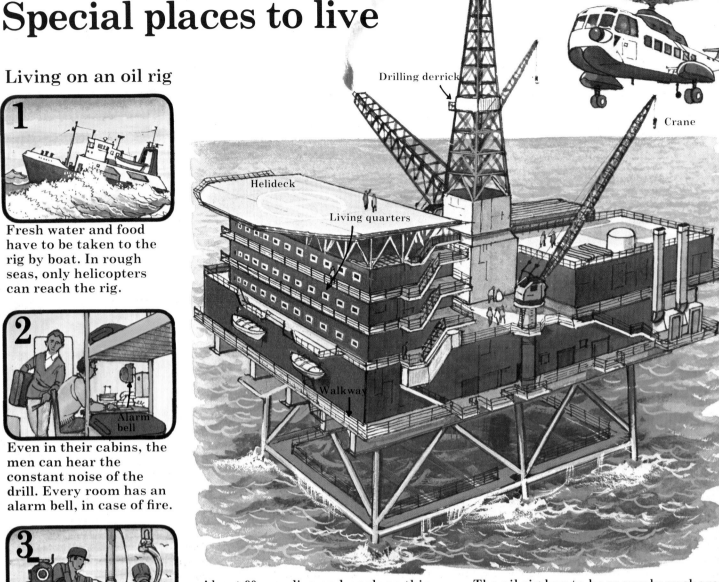

Drilling derrick

Crane

Helideck

Living quarters

Walkway

About 90 men live and work on this oil rig. They spend seven days on the rig, working 12 hour shifts and then fly ashore by helicopter for a week's leave.

The oil rig has to be securely anchored to the sea bed so that it does not break loose in rough seas. Divers regularly check the massive anchors which hold it in place.

Dome house
Domes, like this, have been built by people experimenting with new kinds of houses. They even used old car bodies.

1 ### Zome house
This "Zome" house is heated by the sun. The walls are made of a special material which keeps heat in.

2 Drums filled with water

One wall of the zome is lined with drums filled with water. The sun heats the water and the hot water heats the house.

Lighthouse

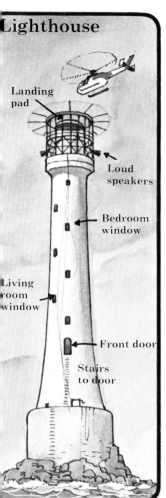

Landing pad

Loud speakers

Bedroom window

Living room window

Front door

Stairs to door

...ll the rooms in a ...ghthouse are round and ...e beds are curved to ... the walls. These have ... be very thick to ...thstand the pounding ... the waves. Three men ...ve here, looking after ...e light and foghorn. ...elicopters land on the ...nding pad on the top ...en in rough weather.

Under the sea

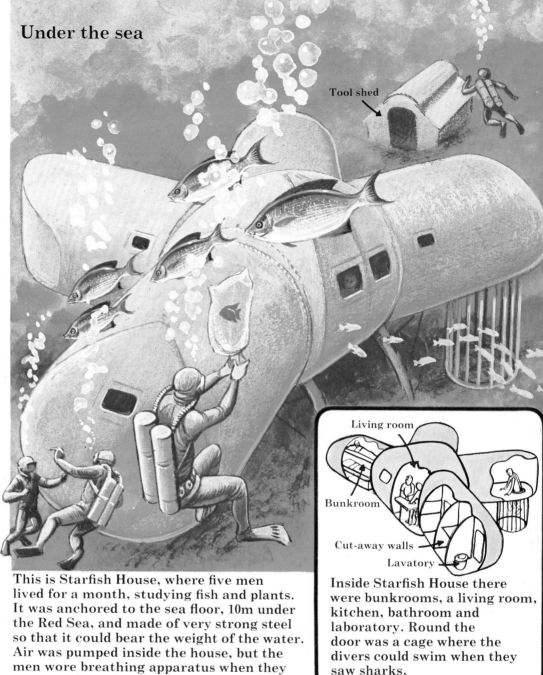

Tool shed

Living room

Bunkroom

Cut-away walls

Lavatory

This is Starfish House, where five men lived for a month, studying fish and plants. It was anchored to the sea floor, 10m under the Red Sea, and made of very strong steel so that it could bear the weight of the water. Air was pumped inside the house, but the men wore breathing apparatus when they swam out into the sea.

Inside Starfish House there were bunkrooms, a living room, kitchen, bathroom and laboratory. Round the door was a cage where the divers could swim when they saw sharks.

Space city

...pace ship from Earth ...ocking into space city.

...the future, people may live in ...ties in space, rather than on the ...owded Earth. This vast space ...ty would spin round so that ...would feel like being on Earth.

Giant mirrors would reflect sunlight into the city and energy from the sun would be used for power and heat. Special screens would protect it from harmful rays.

Inside space city

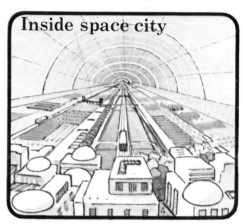

Inside the spokes of space city there would be houses, factories and farmland. There would be air inside the city so people could breathe normally.

Building materials

Stone

Stone makes strong, fire-proof, long-lasting buildings, though it is heavy to lift and transport. Mortar, a mixture of sand, cement* and water, is usually used to hold the stones together. Stones stacked up without mortar make "dry" stone walls.

Quarry where stone is cut from the ground.

House built of roughly cut stones held together with mortar.

"Dry" stone domed roofs on houses in southern Italy.

Concrete

Concrete is a modern building material made of gravel (tiny stones), sand and cement. Mixed with water, it makes a stiff paste which sets hard in hours. When steel rods are added, it is called reinforced concrete and is extremely strong.

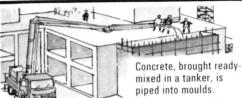
Concrete, brought ready-mixed in a tanker, is piped into moulds.

Ready-made concrete walls are lifted into place by giant cranes.

Bricks

When clay is baked at high temperatures, it becomes very hard. It is used for making building bricks, roof tiles and pipes. Different coloured bricks are made from clays found in different places.

Brick factory where clay is moulded and baked into bricks.

Bricklayers always use mortar to hold bricks in place.

Mud

Mud is plentiful, cheap and easy to work with. It is often mixed with chopped straw to give it extra strength. Some soils bake rock-hard in the sun and may last for hundreds of years, though mud houses need regular repairs.

Mud paste is pressed into wooden moulds and left to dry into bricks.

Dry earth is rammed into hard bricks in this machine.

Houses made of mud bricks held together with mud paste.

Wood

Wood rots easily in damp weather and must be given regular coats of paint or varnish to protect it. It also catches fire easily. In forested places, it is a cheap building material. It is widely used for making roof frames.

Tree trunks are cut into planks at saw mills.

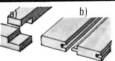
Two ways of joining wood: a) a corner joint, b) planks side-by-side.

House built with smoothed planks of wood in southern U.S.A.

Small house in Canada built of whole logs, joined with nails.

Bamboo, grass and leaves

Bamboo plants grow quickly in hot, wet countries and their stems make a strong and flexible, but very light, building material. Grass, reeds and leaves are light and waterproof too, though when dry they easily catch fire.

House walls made of bamboo poles split lengthways and woven.

African house woven like a giant basket from split bamboo.

House made of tall reeds by Marsh Arab people in Iraq.

Lakeside house in Peru made of reeds sewn in mats.

Wool and skins

People who move around with their herds of animals need light, portable homes. They often make them from animal skins or hair, supported by branches or wooden poles. Unwashed wool contains natural oils which make it waterproof.

Turcoman woman from Iran making tent felt from sheep's wool. The wool is beaten with sticks and rolled so its fibres tangle together into thick felt.

The pieces of felt are stretched over a wood frame to make a large tent called a yurt. Smoke turns the white felts black after a few years.

Building to suit the climate

Here are some of the ways people make their houses suit the climate they live in.

Thick walls keep the heat out in summer and the cold out in winter.

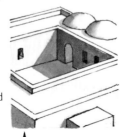
Houses with windows facing a courtyard keep cool and shady.

Pale colours reflect the sun's rays so walls do not absorb their heat.

Shutters made of slats of wood (louvres) let in cool breezes, but keep out the sun's glare.

Wooden shutters protect windows from strong winds and snow-storms.

Windscoops direct wind down into houses in this hot Pakistani town.

*Cement is made from a rock called limestone. It sets very hard when mixed with water.

made of stone slate, which can ...it into thin sheets.

 Grand city house built of smoothed and neatened stone blocks and mortar.

 Paint on walls helps stop stones being worn away by weather.

 House walls made of pebbles or pieces of flint set in mortar.

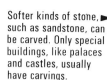 Softer kinds of stone, such as sandstone, can be carved. Only special buildings, like palaces and castles, usually have carvings.

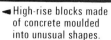 High-rise blocks made of concrete moulded into unusual shapes.

Reinforced concrete is so strong, it can be used to make overhanging roofs and balconies.

Concrete is usually a dull grey colour, but it can be coloured to make towns more attractive.

 made of clay tiles. ...verlap to keep ...e rain.

 These tiles are a different shape—like pipes cut in half.

 Roman brick building. Their bricks were smaller than modern ones.

 Bricks were used a lot for building about 100 years ago.

 Decorated chimneys made by skilled bricklayers.

 Patterned house wall made by using different coloured bricks.

 ...uilt by pouring ...to a wooden

 Four-storey mud brick houses in Saudi Arabia.

 "Cob" house in England. Walls are built of layers of mud paste and straw.

 Houses built by the Masai people of east Africa from cow dung.

 Houses in Morocco built with mud bricks made in patterned moulds.

 Mud house in Nigeria which has been painted.

 ...pping planks, ...weather-boards, ...this house.

 Timber frame house, with walls filled in with bricks.

 Frame for jungle house made with naturally forked branches.

 House in Burma built by weaving thin strips of wood together.

 Roof of wooden tiles, called "shingles". It is steep so rain runs off.

 Carved wood is often used to decorate houses, even brick or stone ones.

 ...rass house made ...ng mats over a ...of branches.

 House in Ethiopia being covered with waterproof bamboo leaves.

 Palm leaves being knotted together ready for making a roof.

 House with finished palm leaf roof, called palm thatch.

 Roof being thatched with bundles of straw or reeds.

 House in Europe with straw thatch. It is steep so rain runs off.

 ...n women weave ...rips of cloth for ...ents from a

mixture of sheep's wool and goat hair.

 The woven strips are sewn together to make the walls and roof of 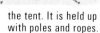 the tent. It is held up with poles and ropes.

 The Lapps use reindeer skins to make their tents. The skins are stitched together and stretched over a hollow cone of branches tied together at the top.

In some hot countries, wire mesh is put over windows to keep out insects.

Flat roofs are common in hot, dry places. They make a cool place for sleeping at night.

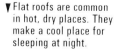 Thick rounded roofs on houses in Greece keep out summer heat.

 Gently sloping roofs hold a blanket of snow which keeps house warm.

In places where it rains a lot, roofs are often steep so it runs off.

Jutting-out roofs protect walls from rain and provide shelter.

 In hot, wet places, stilts protect houses from flooding and allow cooling breezes to blow under them.

Going further

Books to read

Houses round the world:
Wigwams, Igloos and Bungalows by Elizabeth Hogarth (Piccolo)
Houses and Homes by Carolyn Cooke (Macdonald)
Homes in Australia by Unstead and Henderson (Black)
Seen in Britain by Henry Pluckrose (Mills and Boon)
Looking Around in Town and Country by Philip Sauvain (Watts)
National Geographic magazine (National Geographic Society) sometimes has good pictures of peoples' houses and homes. You can find it in reference libraries and in second-hand book shops.
Macdonald Countries series (Macdonald)
Looking at Other Countries series (Black)

Houses through the ages:
Homes by Molly Harrison (Ernest Benn)

Building houses:
How your House Works by Brian Read (Transworld)
Building a House by Brian Read (Transworld)

Places to visit

Britain:
Museum of Mankind, London, sometimes has special exhibitions about peoples' houses.
The Commonwealth Institute, London, has displays on a the Commonwealth countries.
The Avoncroft Museum of Buildings in Bromsgrove, Worcestershire, has reconstructed Iron Age huts and old English houses.
St Fagan's Welsh Museum, Cardiff, has reconstructions of old buildings from Wales.

The following museums in Australia, New Zealand and Canada have exhibitions about peoples of the world:
The South Australian Museum, Adelaide, Australia; Canterbury Museum, Christchurch, New Zealand; National Museum of Man, Ottawa, Canada; McCord Museum, Montreal, Canada and Royal Ontario Museum, Toronto, Canada.

Index

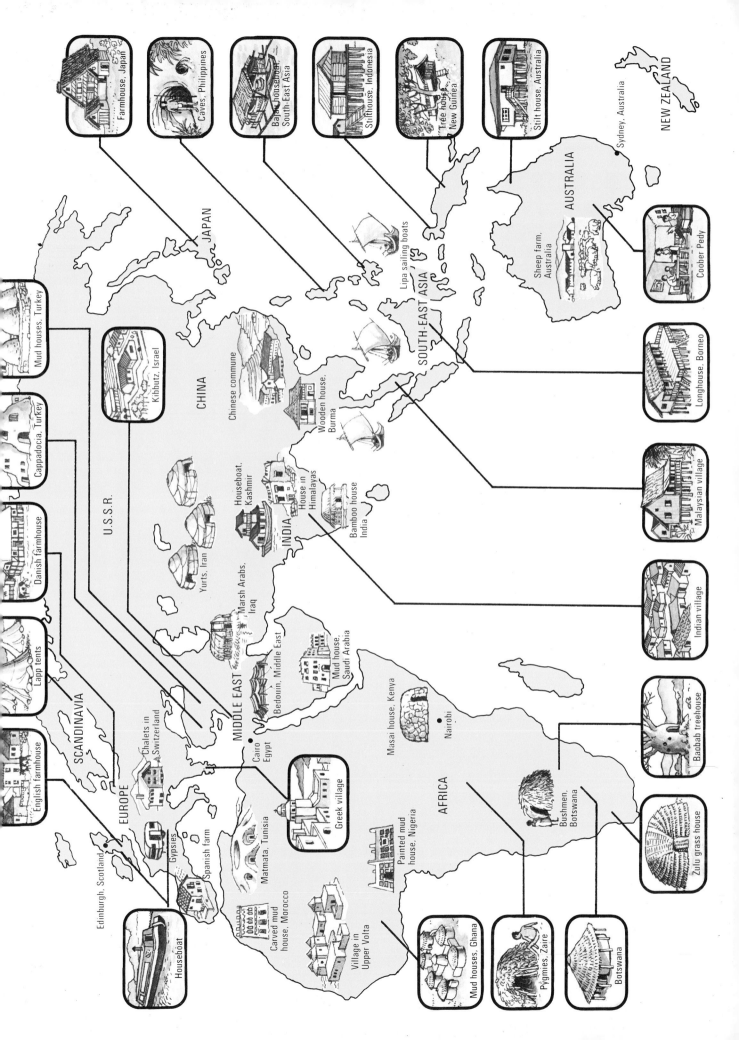

Farmhouse, Japan

Caves, Philippines

Bajau houseboat, South-East Asia

Stilthouse, Indonesia

Tree house, New Guinea

Stilt house, Australia

NEW ZEALAND

Sydney, Australia

AUSTRALIA

Sheep farm, Australia

Coober Pedy

Lipa sailing boats

SOUTH-EAST ASIA

Longhouse, Borneo

Mud houses, Turkey

Kibbutz, Israel

CHINA

JAPAN

Chinese commune

Wooden house, Burma

Malaysian village

Cappadocia, Turkey

U.S.S.R.

Houseboat, Kashmir

House in Himalayas

INDIA

Bamboo house India

Indian village

Danish farmhouse

Yurts, Iran

Marsh Arabs, Iraq

Lapp tents

SCANDINAVIA

Bedouin, Middle East

Mud house, Saudi Arabia

MIDDLE EAST

English farmhouse

Chalets in Switzerland

Cairo Egypt

Masai house, Kenya

Nairobi

Baobab treehouse

EUROPE

Edinburgh, Scotland

Gypsies

Spanish farm

Greek village

AFRICA

Bushmen, Botswana

Houseboat

Matmata, Tunisia

Painted mud house, Nigeria

Zulu grass house

Carved mud house, Morocco

Village in Upper Volta

Mud houses, Ghana

Pygmies, Zaire

Botswana